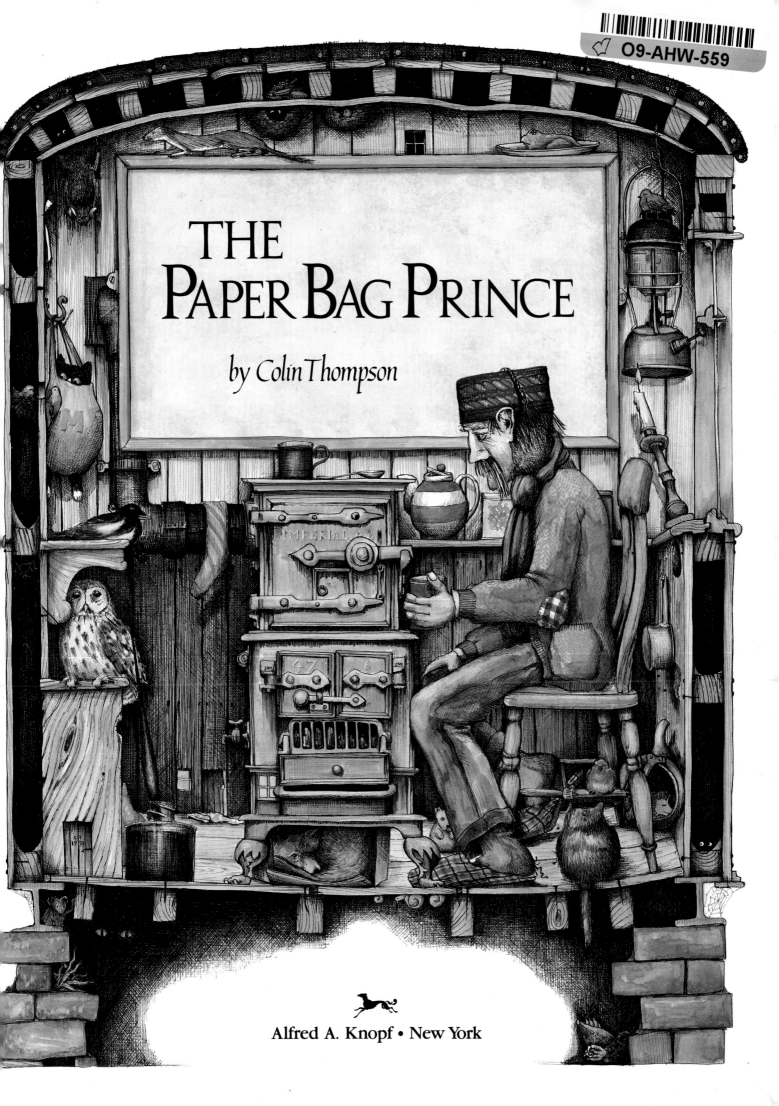

THE PAPER BAG PRINCE

by Colin Thompson

Alfred A. Knopf • New York

THIS IS A BORZOI BOOK
PUBLISHED BY ALFRED A. KNOPF, INC.

Copyright © 1992 by Colin Thompson
All rights reserved under International and Pan-American
Copyright Conventions. Published in the United States by
Alfred A. Knopf, Inc., New York. Distributed by Random House,
Inc., New York. Published in Great Britain by Julia MacRae
Books in 1992. First American Edition, 1992.

Library of Congress Cataloging-in-Publication Data
Thompson, Colin (Colin Edward)
The paper bag prince / by Colin Thompson. p.   cm.
Summary: A wise old man who visits the town dump
every day moves into an abandoned train there
and watches as nature gradually reclaims the polluted land.
ISBN 0-679-83048-0 (trade) — ISBN 0-679-93048-5 (lib. bdg.)
[1. Ecology—Fiction. 2. Pollution—Fiction.]
I. Title.   PZ7.T371424Pap   1992
[E]—dc20   91-27453

Manufactured in Singapore
2 4 6 8 0 9 7 5 3 1

For Heather

Out past the edge of a big untidy town was a beautiful green valley. Hidden behind its tall trees were bright flowers and bushes full of birds. In the middle of this lovely place, the people of the town dumped their rubbish. Every day trucks went down to the end of the narrow lane and dumped the town's leftovers. There should have been a pretty village in the valley, but instead there was a terrible mess.

New rubbish was thrown on top of old rubbish. At the bottom of the pile, dark green moss clung to the seats of cars that had almost vanished into the earth. Between the old cars there were wildflowers growing, and trees had begun to live in the oldest corners of the dump. Nature never gave up. Wherever there was a tiny gap, something green managed to survive.

Animals lived there too, not just mice and insects but larger creatures like cats and weasels and foxes. For them it was a wonderful place, safe from the attentions of people. The twisted, torn bodies of refrigerators, pressing into the flattened frames of old beds, made a hundred little corridors and highways. Under an old clock lazy dormice slept. Inside a television a family of sparrows made their home. There was life everywhere. Even in a tiny puddle in a worn-out shoe there were mosquito larvae watching for summer.

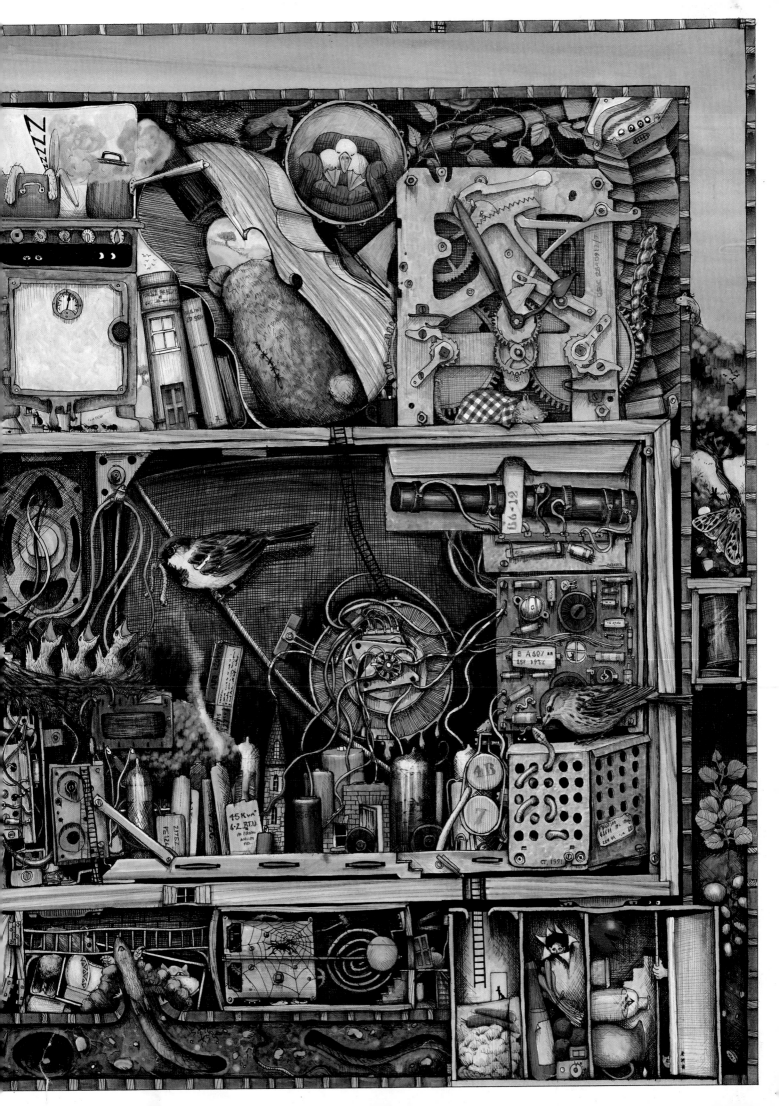

Humans didn't like to be near the rubbish. For them it was a dangerous place, with rusty metal and broken glass and rotting things that smelled of disease. In a back corner there was the Poison Pool, where large metal drums leaked into a brown pond and nothing, not even the smallest plant, could live. The animals were more clever than the people. They kept away from the Poison Pool and thrived in their man-made environment.

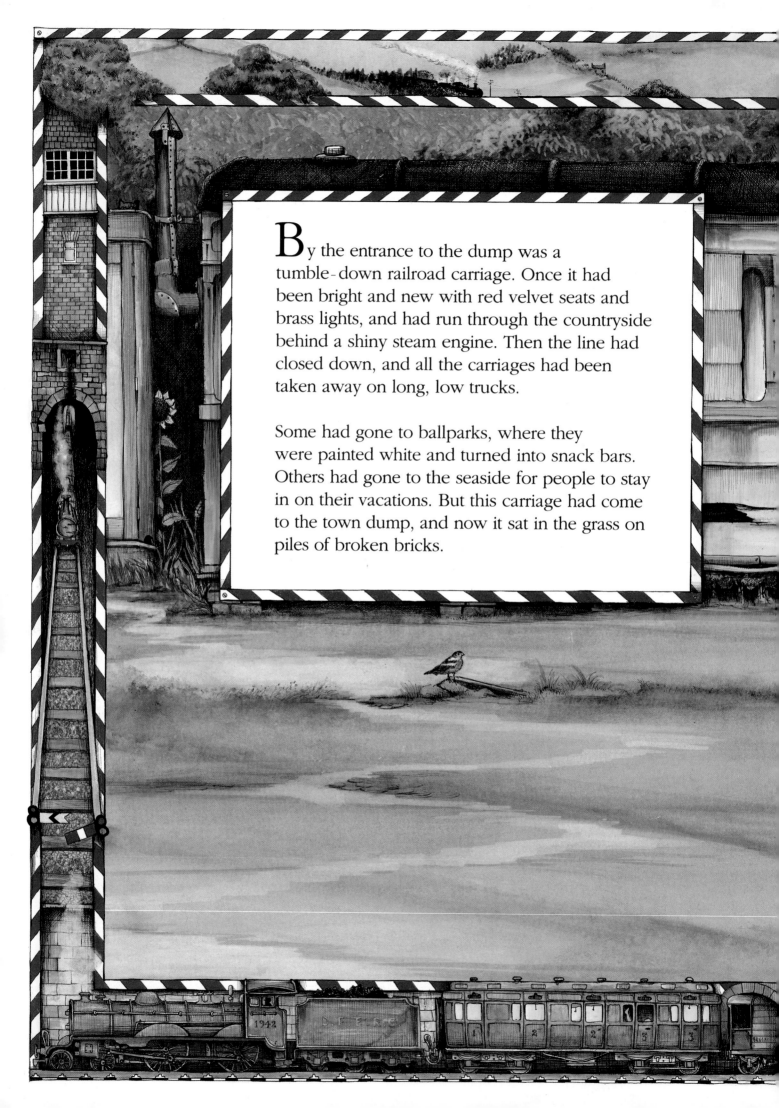

By the entrance to the dump was a
tumble-down railroad carriage. Once it had
been bright and new with red velvet seats and
brass lights, and had run through the countryside
behind a shiny steam engine. Then the line had
closed down, and all the carriages had been
taken away on long, low trucks.

Some had gone to ballparks, where they
were painted white and turned into snack bars.
Others had gone to the seaside for people to stay
in on their vacations. But this carriage had come
to the town dump, and now it sat in the grass on
piles of broken bricks.

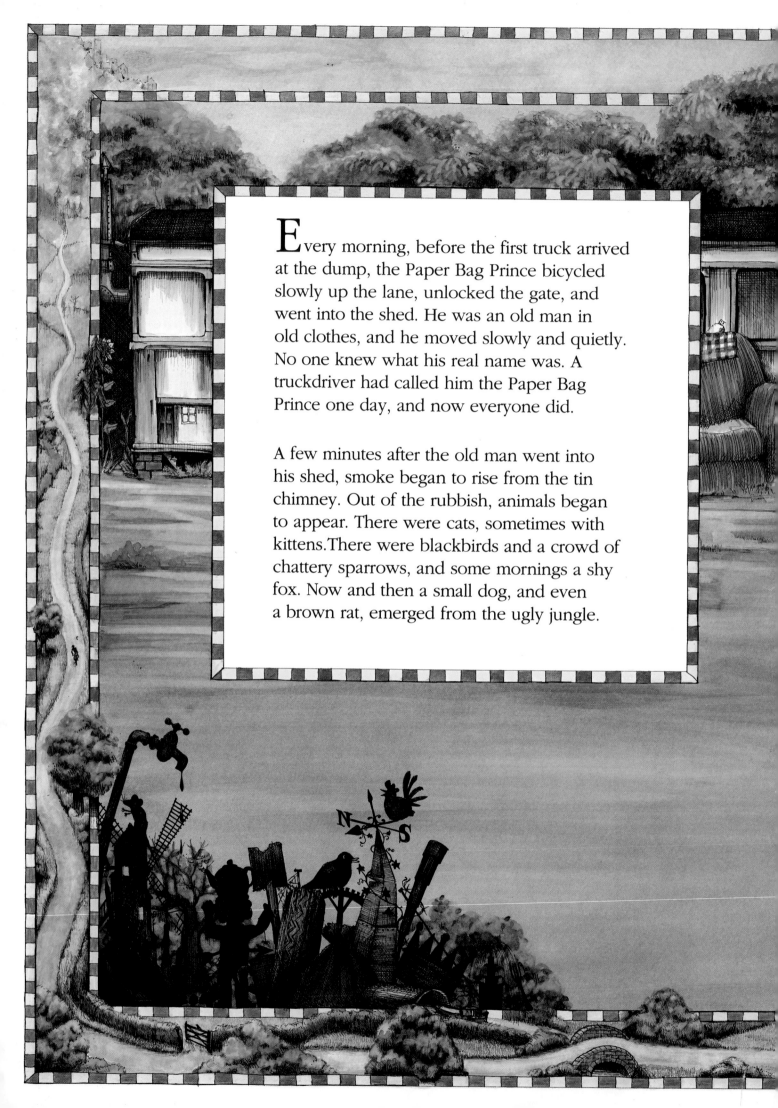

Every morning, before the first truck arrived at the dump, the Paper Bag Prince bicycled slowly up the lane, unlocked the gate, and went into the shed. He was an old man in old clothes, and he moved slowly and quietly. No one knew what his real name was. A truckdriver had called him the Paper Bag Prince one day, and now everyone did.

A few minutes after the old man went into his shed, smoke began to rise from the tin chimney. Out of the rubbish, animals began to appear. There were cats, sometimes with kittens. There were blackbirds and a crowd of chattery sparrows, and some mornings a shy fox. Now and then a small dog, and even a brown rat, emerged from the ugly jungle.

When the stove was alight, the old man came back out and sat down on a chair by the door. Out of a paper bag he brought food. The cats came straight over and rubbed around his legs. The birds hopped onto the back of his chair, where they could keep an eye on the cats. The fox crept up, crawling flat on the ground like a sheepdog. The dog, which didn't come often, was the most nervous of all and kept well back.

"Come on, Princess," the old man said softly. The dog put her head on one side and stayed where she was. She was very thin, and when he threw her food, she ate it as if she hadn't eaten for days. But no matter how he tried, she would never come any closer.

By the time the trucks began to arrive, the animals had vanished back into the rubbish.

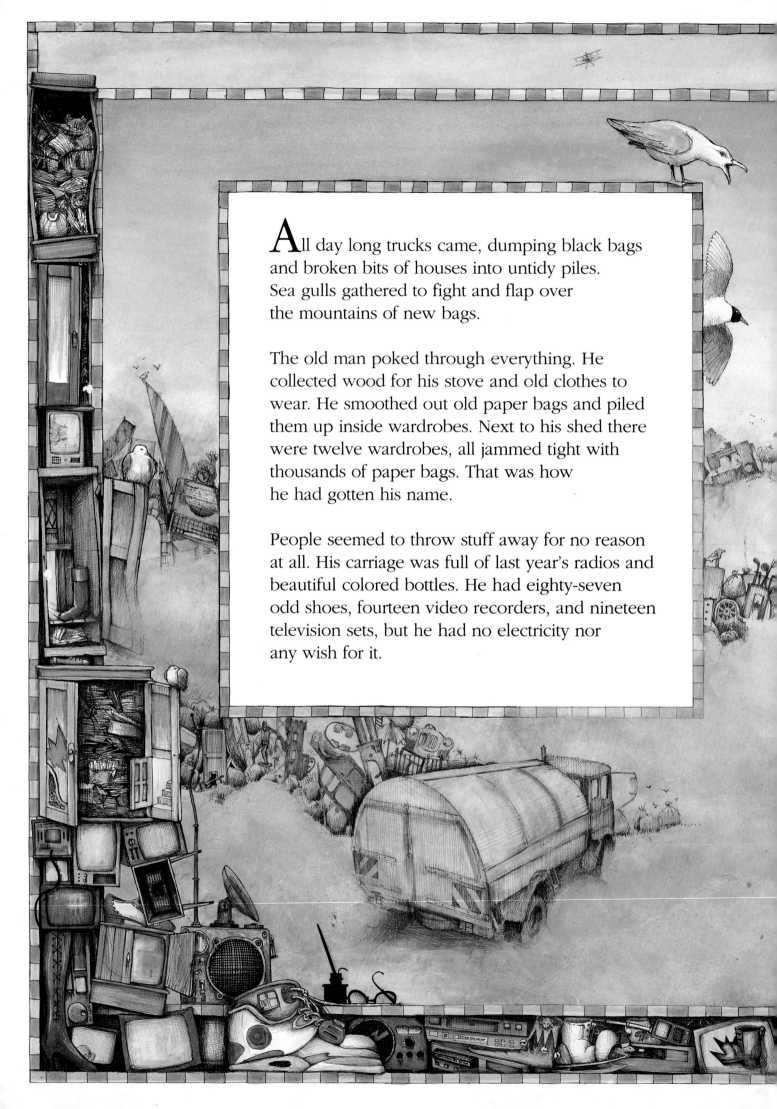

All day long trucks came, dumping black bags and broken bits of houses into untidy piles. Sea gulls gathered to fight and flap over the mountains of new bags.

The old man poked through everything. He collected wood for his stove and old clothes to wear. He smoothed out old paper bags and piled them up inside wardrobes. Next to his shed there were twelve wardrobes, all jammed tight with thousands of paper bags. That was how he had gotten his name.

People seemed to throw stuff away for no reason at all. His carriage was full of last year's radios and beautiful colored bottles. He had eighty-seven odd shoes, fourteen video recorders, and nineteen television sets, but he had no electricity nor any wish for it.

One day the trucks stopped coming.

The Paper Bag Prince sat on his seat in the summer sunshine. A skylark was singing high in the air above him, and along the lane it was silent. There was no thundery rumble of heavy trucks approaching. There was nothing, just the skylark. It was wonderful.

"Perhaps it's a holiday," he said to no one in particular. But it wasn't. He leaned back in his chair, with his face tipped up toward the warm sun, and was soon fast asleep.

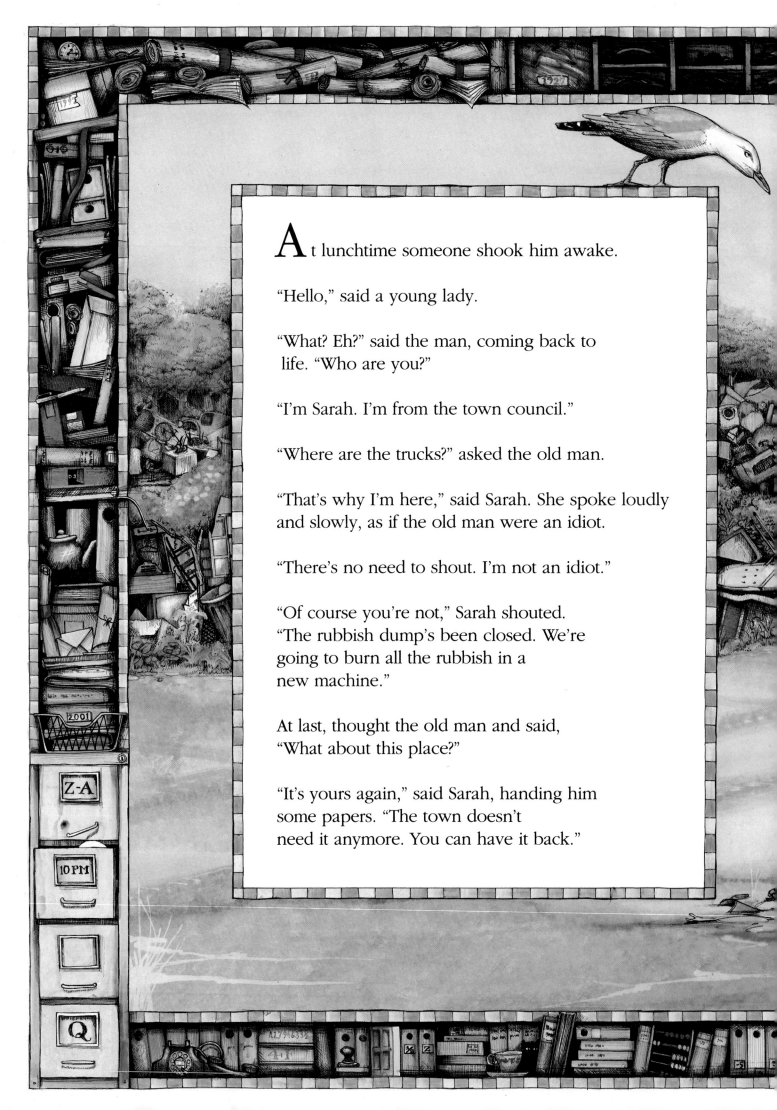

At lunchtime someone shook him awake.

"Hello," said a young lady.

"What? Eh?" said the man, coming back to life. "Who are you?"

"I'm Sarah. I'm from the town council."

"Where are the trucks?" asked the old man.

"That's why I'm here," said Sarah. She spoke loudly and slowly, as if the old man were an idiot.

"There's no need to shout. I'm not an idiot."

"Of course you're not," Sarah shouted. "The rubbish dump's been closed. We're going to burn all the rubbish in a new machine."

At last, thought the old man and said, "What about this place?"

"It's yours again," said Sarah, handing him some papers. "The town doesn't need it anymore. You can have it back."

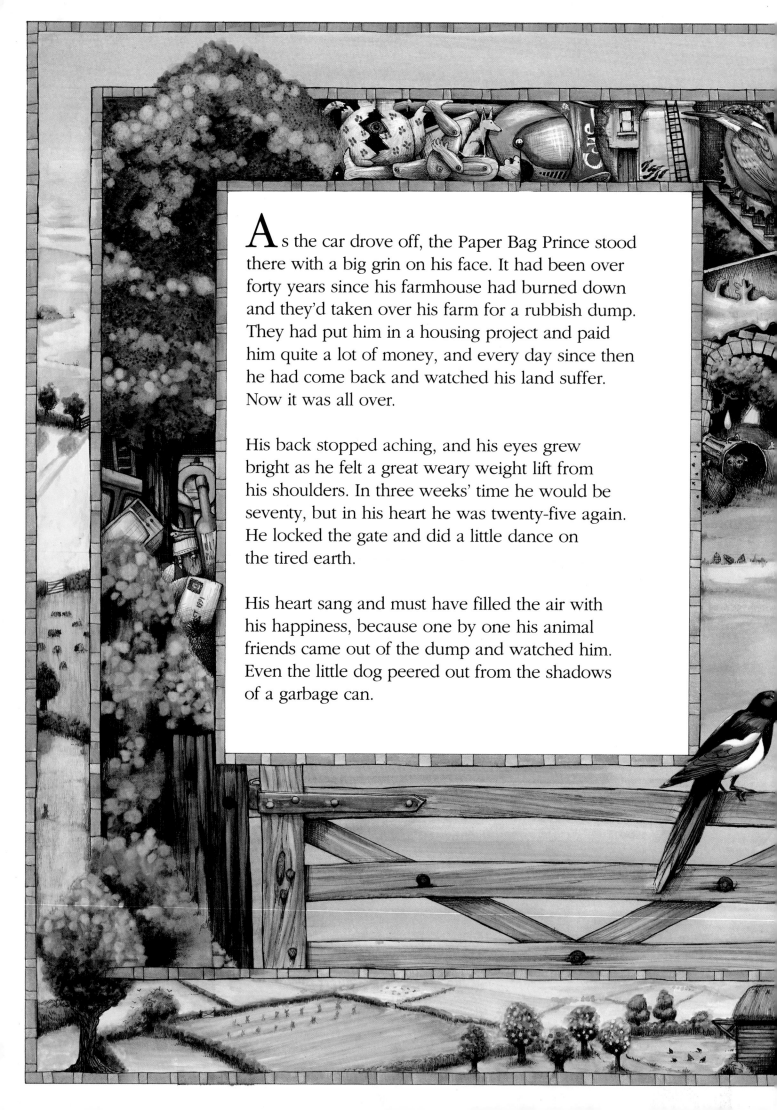

As the car drove off, the Paper Bag Prince stood there with a big grin on his face. It had been over forty years since his farmhouse had burned down and they'd taken over his farm for a rubbish dump. They had put him in a housing project and paid him quite a lot of money, and every day since then he had come back and watched his land suffer. Now it was all over.

His back stopped aching, and his eyes grew bright as he felt a great weary weight lift from his shoulders. In three weeks' time he would be seventy, but in his heart he was twenty-five again. He locked the gate and did a little dance on the tired earth.

His heart sang and must have filled the air with his happiness, because one by one his animal friends came out of the dump and watched him. Even the little dog peered out from the shadows of a garbage can.

He walked around his kingdom, followed by the cats. At the back of the valley, the path was overgrown with brambles. No one had been there for years. Soon it would start to look green again as the last of the rubbish disappeared under grass and bushes.

The Paper Bag Prince climbed up into an old truck. He kept a little camping stove there and all the other things he needed to make a pot of tea.

"I should really be drinking champagne," he said out loud, "on a special day like this. I've never had champagne. I wonder what it's like?"

The gray cat couldn't tell him. She'd never had champagne either.

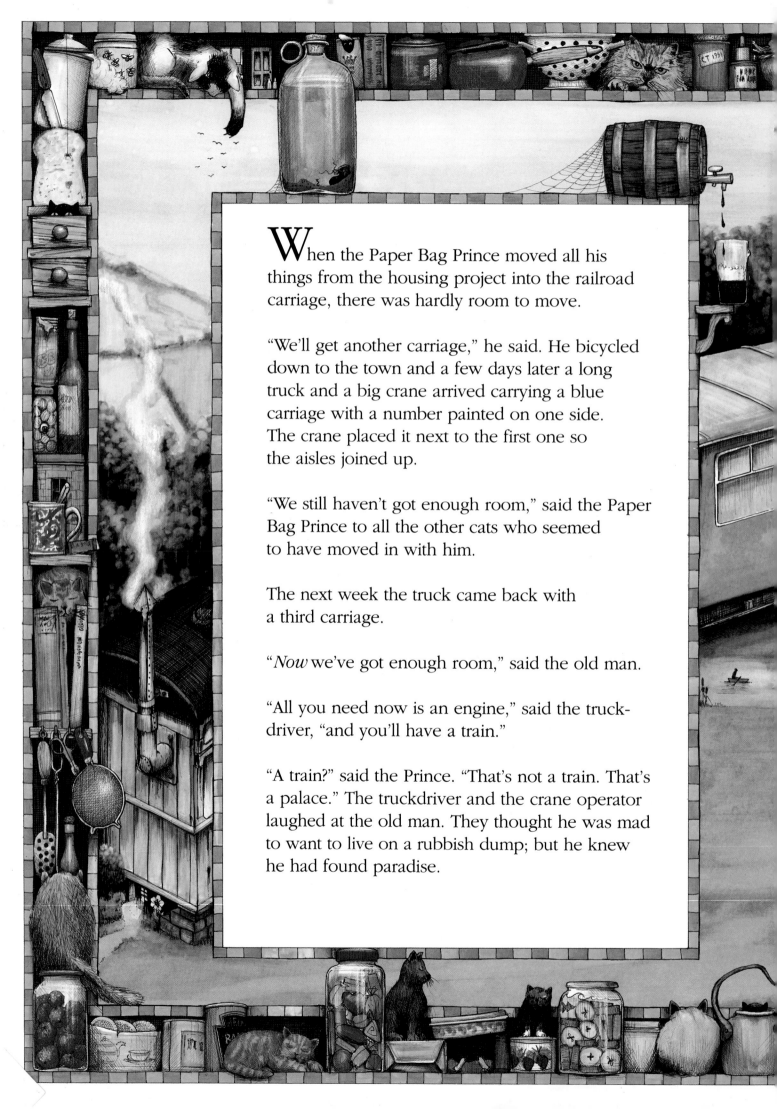

When the Paper Bag Prince moved all his things from the housing project into the railroad carriage, there was hardly room to move.

"We'll get another carriage," he said. He bicycled down to the town and a few days later a long truck and a big crane arrived carrying a blue carriage with a number painted on one side. The crane placed it next to the first one so the aisles joined up.

"We still haven't got enough room," said the Paper Bag Prince to all the other cats who seemed to have moved in with him.

The next week the truck came back with a third carriage.

"*Now* we've got enough room," said the old man.

"All you need now is an engine," said the truck-driver, "and you'll have a train."

"A train?" said the Prince. "That's not a train. That's a palace." The truckdriver and the crane operator laughed at the old man. They thought he was mad to want to live on a rubbish dump; but he knew he had found paradise.

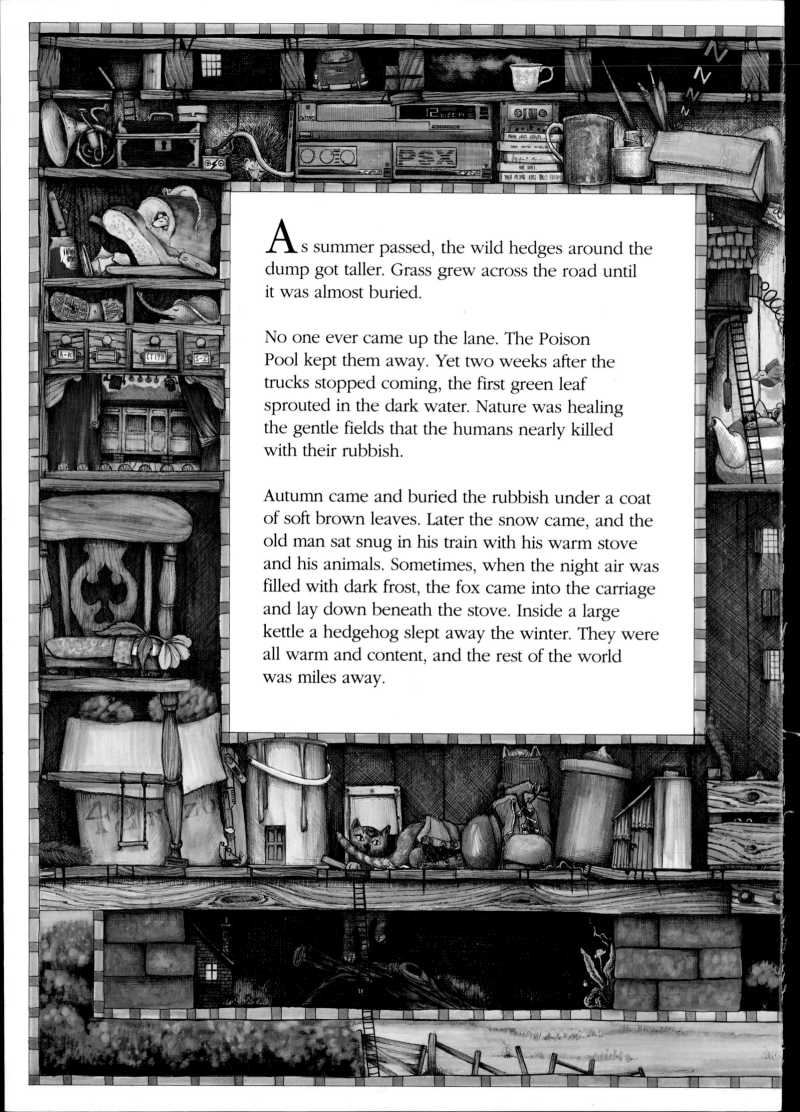

As summer passed, the wild hedges around the dump got taller. Grass grew across the road until it was almost buried.

No one ever came up the lane. The Poison Pool kept them away. Yet two weeks after the trucks stopped coming, the first green leaf sprouted in the dark water. Nature was healing the gentle fields that the humans nearly killed with their rubbish.

Autumn came and buried the rubbish under a coat of soft brown leaves. Later the snow came, and the old man sat snug in his train with his warm stove and his animals. Sometimes, when the night air was filled with dark frost, the fox came into the carriage and lay down beneath the stove. Inside a large kettle a hedgehog slept away the winter. They were all warm and content, and the rest of the world was miles away.

The days got shorter and shorter. It was nearly Christmas. The old man walked through the trees toward the old truck. He had forgotten to shut the cab door, and the seats were covered with snow. As he climbed in to brush it out, something jumped up out of a pile of leaves. It was the little dog. With no new rubbish to scavenge through, she had grown even thinner and was too weak to run away.

"Come on, Princess," said the old man, "there's no need to be afraid."

He put her inside his coat and carried her back home. He fed her and brushed her and tucked her into his bed. More snow fell during the night, but in the morning the sky was blue from side to side, and the thin sun shone down on the best Christmas the Paper Bag Prince and the little dog had ever known.